Sissy and Me

DIANNE BASSETT-GIEHTBROCK

AuthorHouse™
1663 Liberty Drive
Bloomington, IN 47403
www.authorhouse.com
Phone: 1-800-839-8640

First published by AuthorHouse 6/14/2011

ISBN: 978-1-4567-6943-7 (sc)

Library of Congress Control Number: 2011907909

Printed in the United States of America

Any people depicted in stock imagery provided by Thinkstock are models,
and such images are being used for illustrative purposes only.
Certain stock imagery © Thinkstock.

This book is printed on acid-free paper.

authorHOUSE®

This book is dedicated to my always supportive and loving husband Eric and our two beautiful daughters, Paige and Chloe. Without them there would be no inspiration for my story. It is an honor to have such a supportive partner by my side, always telling me to chase my dreams. Without you this wouldn't be possible. To my little ladies, whose continuous daily laughter fuels my desire to write. May you always follow your dreams and chase happiness. To my mom and dad, my foundation and solid ground, thank you for being so close, in distance and in heart. To my brother Steve, my favorite sibling who I have learned so much from, our relationship I cherish. To my buddy Ava, my "Editor in Chief", thanks for all of your help and support. To all of my family and friends, this wouldn't be possible without all of your love and support. Thank you.

"Mom! She's copying me!"

Honey, that's what little sisters do. She does what you do because she looks up to you. She wants to be like you. Take that as a compliment. She loves you.

"Mom! She's staring at me. Tell her to stop!"

Honey, that's what little sisters do. She thinks you are beautiful. Take that as a compliment and know that she loves you.

"Mom! She's laughing at me!"

Honey, that's what little sisters do. She thinks that you are funny. She is laughing with you, not at you. Take that as a compliment. She loves you.

"Mom! She is hurting my feelings. She is laughing and dancing around, and I just fell and hurt myself!"

Honey, that's what little sisters do. That is her way of trying to make you feel better. She sees that you are hurt. She loves you and hates to see you hurting. Take that as a compliment. She loves you.

"Mom! She's writing on my picture and coloring all over it!"

Honey, that's what little sisters do. It's her way of adding to your beautiful picture. She wants to be a part of your creation. She wants to be like you. That should make your heart smile. Take that as a compliment. She loves you.

"Mom! She just bit me!"

Honey, that is what little sisters do when they are pretending. She is pretending to be a kitty cat. You have to be patient and she will eventually learn not to bite. She likes pretending with you. Take that as a compliment. She loves you.

"Mom look, she's drawing a picture with fingers! I draw pictures with fingers too! I taught her that!"

Good! She watches what you do and then copies you. As she copies you, she learns how to be good at things. She loves you more than you know.

"Mom look, she's writing her name! I taught her that!"

That's wonderful! You are such a good teacher. She loves learning from you.

"Mom, she's leaving. Does she have to go?"

Chloe honey, she is a big girl now. She is going into Kindergarten. Instead of feeling sad, you should feel proud of her. You both will have new adventures as you grow up and that should always make your heart smile.

Background on the characters (my daughters)

Paige is a five year old big sister who is going into Kindergarten. She frequently becomes upset with her little sister's intentions. Chloe is three years old and ADORES her big sister. She wants to do everything "just like Paige". The two are inseparable and for the most part love being together. They often need helpful reminders for co-existing as siblings.

This book is written to help young children of all ages learn how to relate to their siblings, find patience and feel love from confusing situations during those young years at home.

CPSIA information can be obtained
at www.ICGtesting.com
Printed in the USA
LVIC040029190412

278046LV00003BA